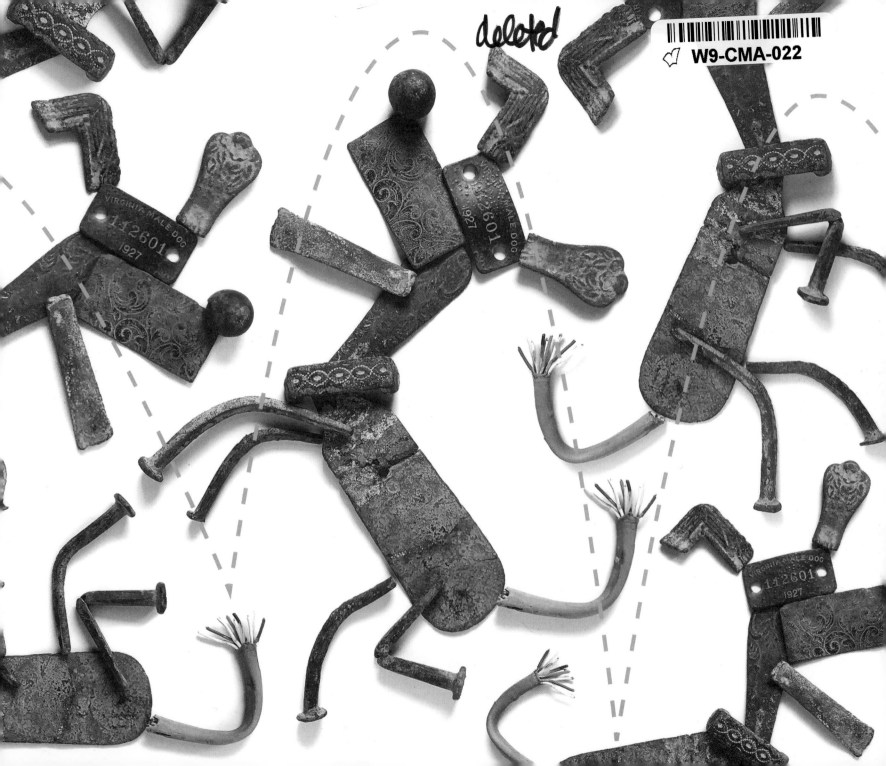

Tag

AND THE

Magic Squeaker

by Sam Hundley

CAPSTONE EDITIONS
a capstone imprint

Published by Capstone Editions,
an imprint of Capstone.
1710 Roe Crest Drive
North Mankato, Minnesota 56003
capstonepub.com

**Library of Congress Cataloging-in-Publication Data is available
on the Library of Congress website.**
ISBN: 9781684464265 (hardcover)
ISBN: 9781684464715 (eBook PDF)

Summary: Tag the dog can do all kinds of things with his squeaker ball—chew it, toss it, and
especially squeak it. Then one day, the squeaker comes to life! Tag is delighted, but the resident
cat is suspicious. Where the cat sees a mystery, Tag sees only magic. Which one is right?

Design Elements: Shutterstock/area381, Shutterstock/Janno Loide

Designed by Sarah Bennett

Printed and bound in the China. 4545

For my mother, Joy

—SH

Tag is a master
with the squeaker ball.

He tosses it up in the air . . .

...then he catches it.

He dribbles it like a basketball . . .

thump   thump   THUMP!

...and he rolls it with his snout.

Uh-oh . . .

"Goodbye, NOISY squeaker," said the cat. "And good riddance!"

A mouse heard the ruckus. He crept out of his hiding place to investigate.

When he saw a hole in the squeaker, he got an idea.

The squeaker rolled
back out from under the couch.

"It's MAGIC!" said Tag.

What??? thought the cat.

"Hi, Tag!" said the squeaker.

"You squeak
AND you talk?"
said Tag.

"New skill,"
said the squeaker.
"Listen, I have
an idea...."

Tag followed
the squeaker's
instructions.

He ran to the
kitchen and tossed it
up onto the counter.

Presto!
Down flew
a tasty dog treat.

CRUNCH

CRUNCH

CRUNCH

Then the squeaker flew down.

Tag jumped up and caught it.

Ta-da!

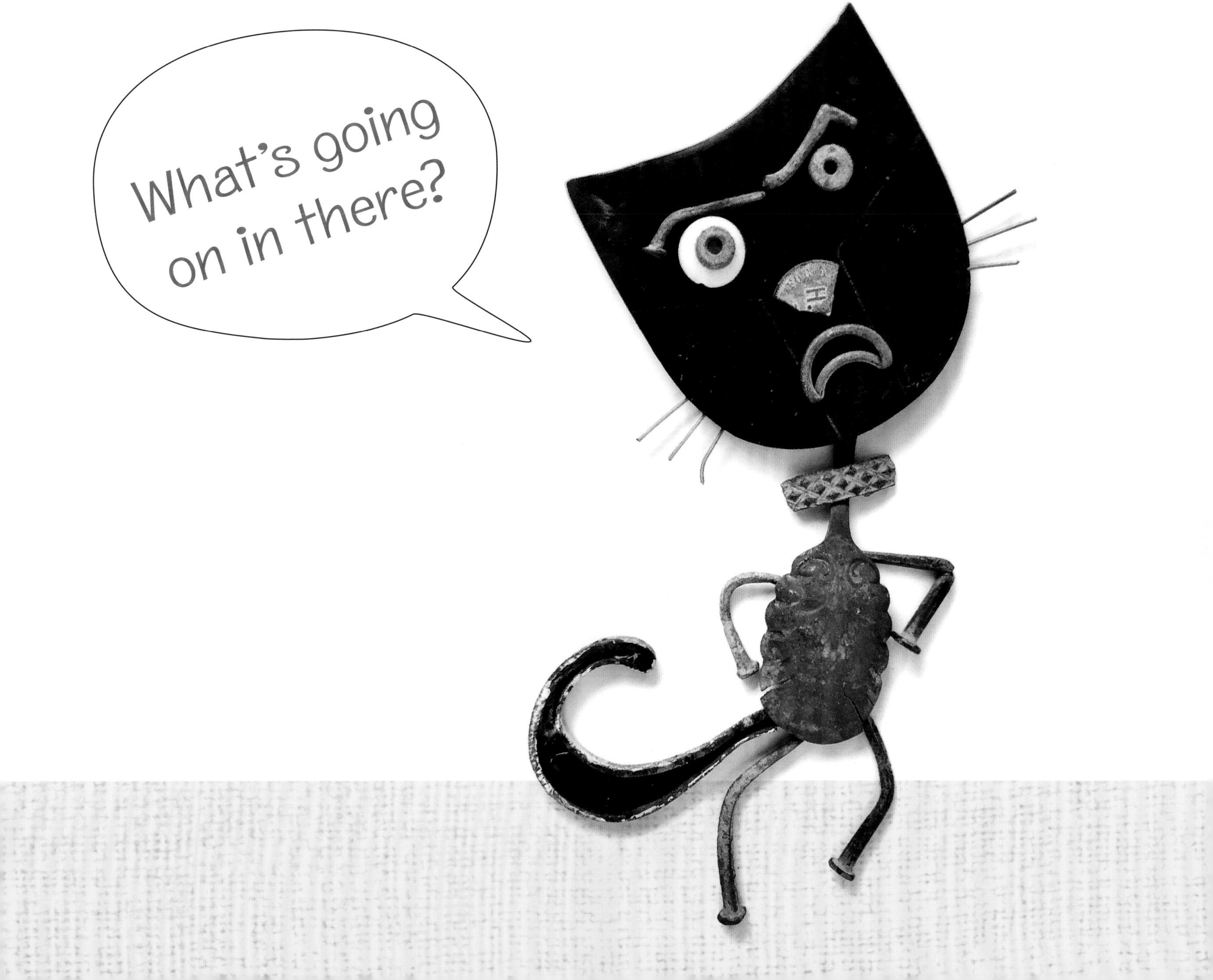
What's going on in there?

"The Magic Squeaker gave me a tasty dog treat," explained Tag.

I see what's going on here,
thought the cat.

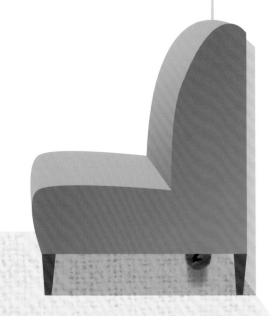

"It's . . . empty?" said the cat. "How can that be?"

"What just happened?" asked Tag.

"I guess it really is a Magic Squeaker," answered the cat.

"Abracadabra," squeaked the mouse.

CRUNCH CRUNCH CRUNCH

About the Artist

Sam Hundley is an American scrap artist who uses found objects that he collects wherever he goes. "Beautiful things are all around us," he says. "And there's no limit to what they can become in one's imagination."

Retired after 39 years as a newspaper artist, Sam now resides in Norfolk, Virginia, with his wife, Lynndale, and their squeaker-loving beagle, Theo, upon whom Tag is based. "Theo is an amazing juggler with his squeaker ball," says Sam. "But when it rolls under the couch, he howls like a baby until I retrieve it!" (See a photo of Theo on the following page.)

Sam's first children's book, *Gifts of the Magpie*, was published in 2021.

About the Art

Almost all of the objects used in creating the illustrations in this book are dug relics—old metal fragments from the 1800s that were unearthed by treasure hunters using metal detectors and shovels. It's hard work, but they do it for the love of discovery. Three of Sam's friends in particular generously donated relics, for which he is so grateful. Thank you, Roy Bahls, Vicky Friedrichs, and Keith Carawan!

That greenish color on the dug relics is called verdigris (pronounced VER-dih-gree). It forms on the surfaces of copper, brass, and bronze over many years of exposure to the elements. It's what gives the characters *character*!

Digging into Sam's Art

1. What do you think was used to make the cat's head?

2. What about the cat's tail?

3. Can you guess what the mouse's ears are made of? (They are more than a century old!)

4. What do you think Tag's tears are made of?

5. Did you figure out why the dog's name is Tag? (Hint: Look at the piece that makes his eyes.)

More Head Scratchers

- Do you think either Tag or the mouse could have achieved the same goal on their own?

- What animal would you like to team up with? What skills would complement yours? Not very tall? A giraffe might help. Can't swim? A dolphin could teach you. Have an early bedtime? An owl can stay up late and help solve a problem. Different skills make for a better team!

ANSWERS 1. the heel of a shoe 2. a metal 2 from a house number 3. flat buttons made of brass 4. bits of sea glass from the Chesapeake Bay 5. Tag's head is made from a dog tag from 1927!

Meet Theo, the talented beagle who inspired this story, with his beloved squeaker ball.

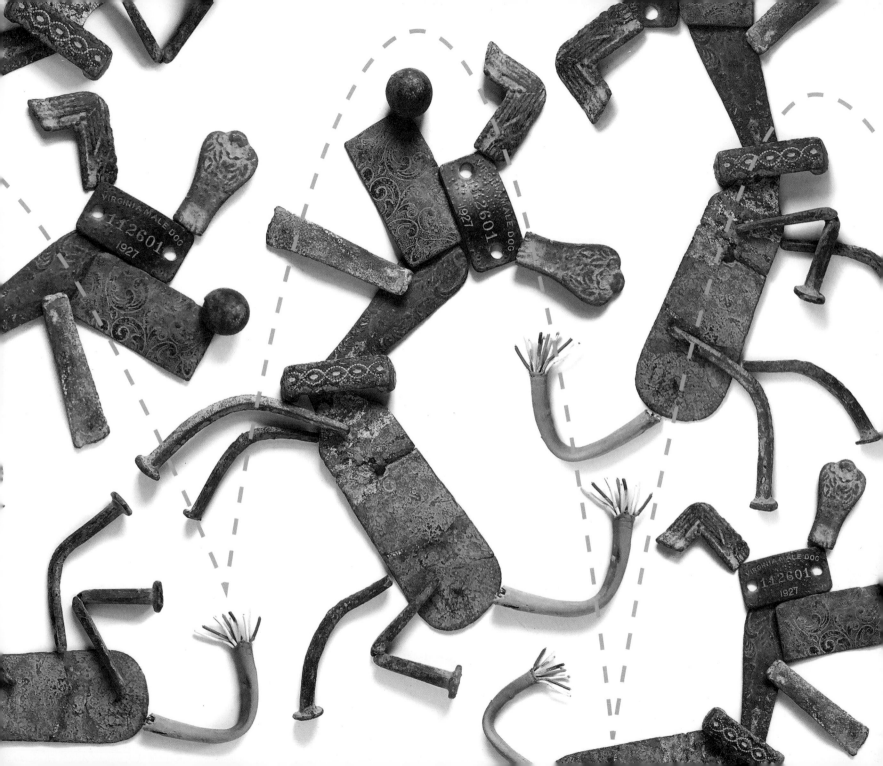